Mama's Bed

Written by   Illustrated by

Jo Ellen Bogart ~ Sylvie Daigneault

Scholastic Canada Ltd.

*To my siblings, Susan,
Cathy and Keith.*

J.E.B.

*To Lise and Guy
S.D.*

The illustrations for this book were drawn
with coloured pencils on paper of various colours.

Canadian Cataloguing in Publication Data

Bogart, Jo Ellen, 1945 -
    Mama's bed

ISBN 0-590-74312-0

I. Daigneault, Sylvie. II. TItle.

PS8553.O53M36 1994   jC813'.54   C95-930252-2
PZ7.B64Ma 1994

8 7 6 5 4 3 2 1   Printed in Canada   5 6 7 8/ 9

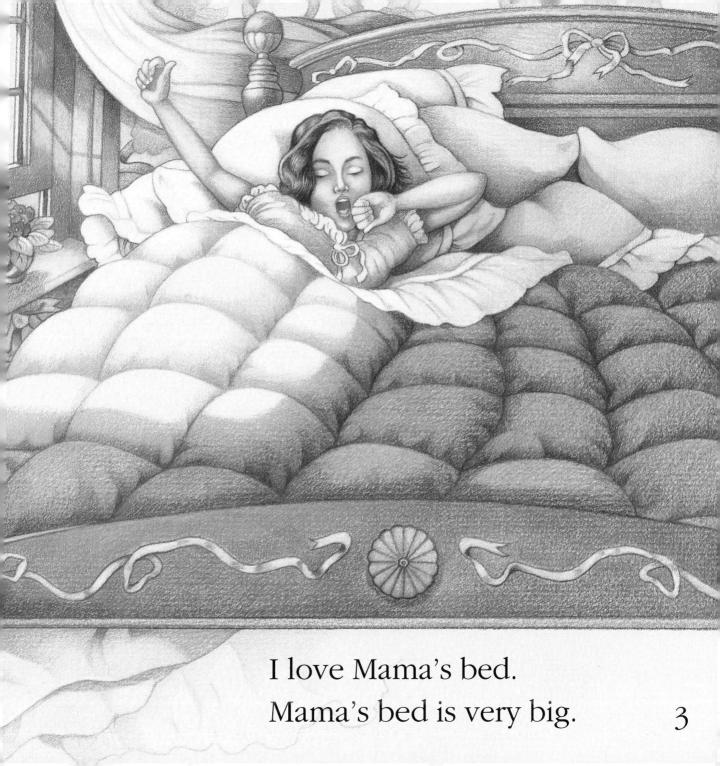

I love Mama's bed.
Mama's bed is very big.

3

4

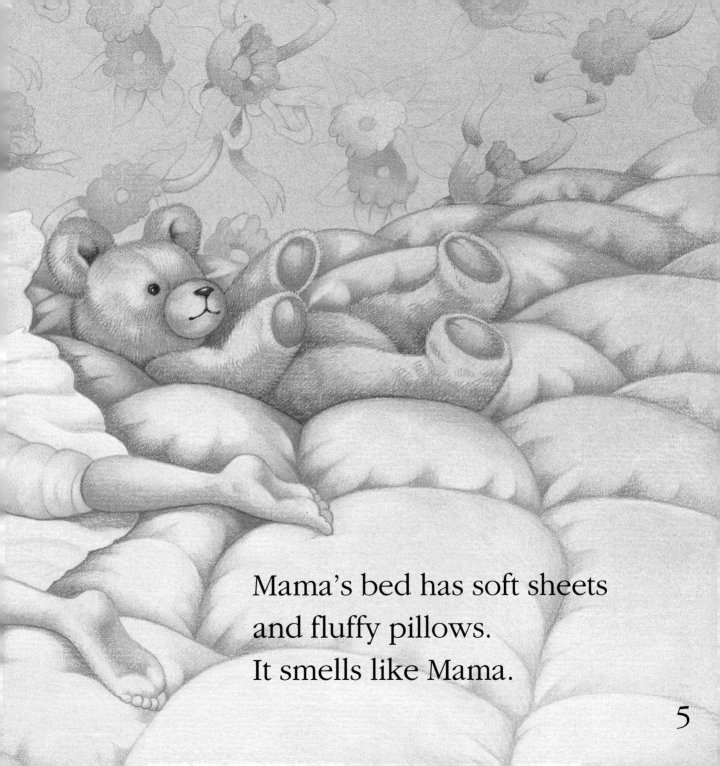

Mama's bed has soft sheets
and fluffy pillows.
It smells like Mama.

6

Mama's bed is cosy
on Sunday morning.
My big sister loves Mama's bed.
Snicker and Puff love Mama's bed, too.

7

On Mama's birthday, we
bring her breakfast in bed.
I had breakfast in Mama's bed
when I was a baby, she says.

9

10

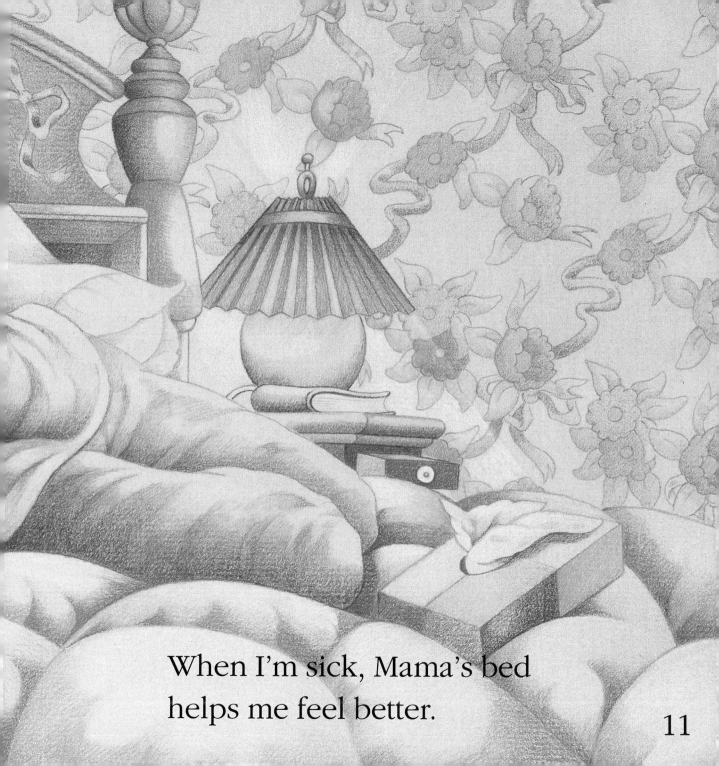

When I'm sick, Mama's bed
helps me feel better.

11

Mama's bed is safe when there is something scary.

12

13

14

Mama's bed is quiet when I feel sad.

15

Mama cut out my teddy bear suit
on her bed.

16

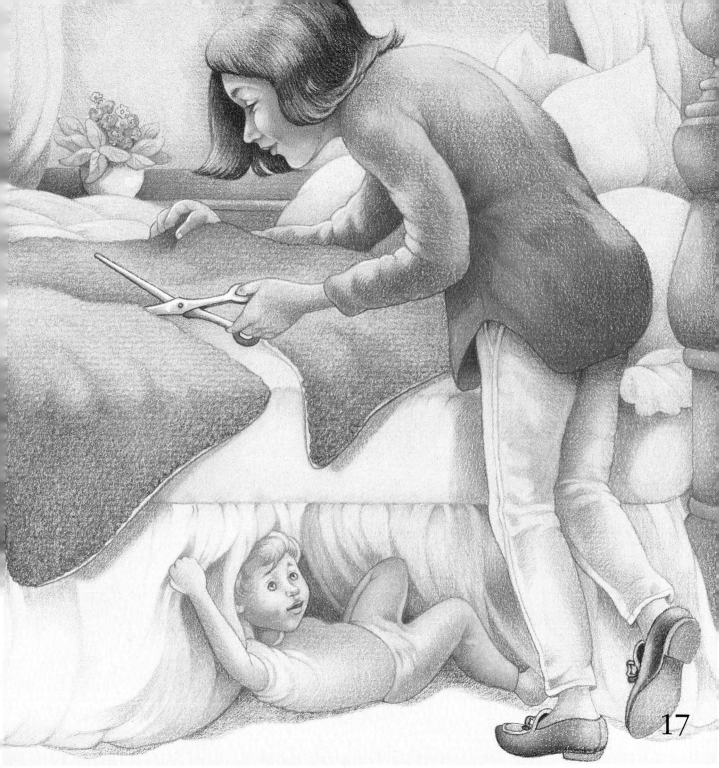

17

Mama's bed is bouncy when I'm happy.

18

19

I help Mama fold the clean
laundry on her bed.

I love Mama's bed on rainy days.

23

Mama loves her bed too,
almost as much as she loved
her own mama's bed.